Autumn
of the
Spring Chicken

Wit and Wisdom
for Women in Midlife

Sue Patton Thoele

Conari Press
Berkeley, California

Dedication

For the many wonderful
women with whom I am sharing
the mysteries, miracles, and
mischief of midlife

Printed in the United States of America on recycled paper
Cover: Sharon Smith Design;
Illustrations: Catherine Rose Crowther

ISBN: 0-943233-47-X

Contents

Acknowledgments

An enormous thank-you to my women friends with whom I have celebrated the hard-earned freedoms of maturing into midlife, as well as moaned, groaned, and giggled over the vicissitudes of aging. Without you the autumn of *this* spring chicken would not be half the rich treasure trove that it is. Each of you is so special to me! A big hug-filled thank-you to Gene, my husband and partner, whose eyesight is thankfully diminishing in direct proportion to the relaxation of my youthful tautness. Special gratitude to my talented and patient publishers, Julie Bennett and Mary Jane Ryan, whose encouragement and support allow me to follow my heart as I write. And yet again, I stand in awe of the Muse who continues to whisper quietly in my ear.

Introduction

Midlife is not the dreaded decline that I feared it would be when I gazed at it from the invincible portals of youth. Rather, midlife is exhilarating and liberating—a time of freedom, creativity, and belly laughs. To be sure, there is also sadness and frustration—loved ones die, economic security is sometimes iffy, and health is not as sure a thing as it used to be—but maturity and an ever-deepening philosophic acceptance of the natural ebb and flow of things can be one of the major perks of midlife (which probably extends from forty to seventy-five or so depending on genes and lifestyle).

Although I've dabbled in poetry since I was a child, I see these verses as "soul snacks," often wrenched from the heights and depths of my being, heart songs and gut groans written in order to sort out my thoughts, pains, and inspirations. The vast majority of *Autumn of the Spring Chicken* has been written since I turned fifty—a major milestone for me. Much of it overflowed from the fullness and excitement I have found in this newly discovered land of "Wow!-I-feel-so-good-about-myself."

We may protest, but I believe all of us have a smidgen of comical and/or mystical poet within. Little limericks or lyrical sonnets float through our minds but we let them drift away on the tide of busyness or lack of attention. Because writing is such a satisfying way to express and clarify our inner processes, I invite you to catch and preserve some of your own thoughts and send them to me at the address listed in the Personal Note at the back of the book. Who knows, we may *all* create another volume!

One of the biggest values of reading is the recognition of ourselves in another's words. As the author voices his or her trials and triumphs, disillusionments and delights, we see our own illuminated and realize that we are not alone. From the safety of this recognition we can open our arms and hearts to embrace and nurture ourselves as well as others, to cultivate the seeds of love for a greater harvest of compassion.

I hope that *Autumn of the Spring Chicken* rings a bell with you, provides a dollop of levity, and helps you feel connected to the wonderful sisterhood of women who are dancing into and through this mysterious and miraculous process of midlife.

Blooming into
Our Best Selves

Autumn of the Spring Chicken

I feel as feisty and fluffy
                as a chick.
But walking up stairs to the sound
            of gravel-filled knee joints
And the fact that I am equally interested
                 in whether the rooster will
                     find me desirable
As I am in his retirement plan,
Reminds me graphically
          that autumn has finally come
               to this spring chicken.

Recollections of a '60s Housewife

Berkeley in the sixties
        mecca for change.
Living (fairer to say, *existing*!)
Only sixty short miles away
I pursed my lips
Turned out a good meal
        but a deaf ear
And did what I thought
        was expected of me.
Dutifully I wore my sturdy
        nursing bra
Never dreaming of washing it
        in hot water
Let alone
    burning it!
Changing diapers, not philosophies
Dedicated to security,
       not service
Hiding from what I knew.

Afraid of . . .
Afraid of *what?*
      Almost anything
        practically everything.
"What will THEY think?"
Luckily, all my fears came true
And, in the crucible of insecurity,
         I was reborn

Able to have opinions of my own
Willing to *think*.

Now my son studies at Berkeley
And I wear hippie garb
                to costume parties
Reminding me that
Although I played The Housewife
                        in the sixties
Only I hold the blueprint
                for my life
And it is constantly
            being revised.

Going Solo

I always thought
         I would breeze
                  through life
On a bicycle
       built for two.
And here I am
       surprised
           and chagrined
Laboriously
      pedaling uphill
             solo!
For this I need
       training wheels
And the wind
     at my back!

Overcoming

Twisting
     turning
         clawing
             scratching
Vowing, struggling, praying
Inching upward
Breaking the surface!

Freeing myself from the
         pit of negativity
And self-condemnation

Overcoming

Breathing freely
        and with love
Looking upon others
        with trust
           and affection

As I look back
      on where
         I have been
I give thanks
      for where
         I have come
And look forward
      to where
         I am going

Christmas Letter from
Someone You May Know

Holiday greetings
            from the Mental Rehab Ward
Where I have finally
            found some serenity and quiet!
This year has found us embroiled
                in the empty-nesters' nightmare.

Two of our three adult kids
                flew back to the
                    heretofore peaceful nest
Bringing music, laundry, appetites,
                        and angst.
Our other child
        lives an alternative lifestyle
                marginally employed and
                    precariously healthy.

As the months wore on
            my mother-welcoming-smile
                turned to teeth-crushing clenches,
Blood pressure elevated
                mood deflated.

Father handled privacy invasion
                        wisely
Leaving on his vacated pillow
                a hand-tied fishing fly

As clue to his
        coping strategy.
The golden years
        seemed to be tarnishing.

Meanwhile,
        here in the hospital,
I have resolved
        that *this* year
I will
     give up *worrying*.

Happy New Year!

Waiting in the Wood

The wood is dark
        crisp leaves
            whisper around my ankles.
I don't know
      which direction to take
I don't even know
       exactly where I'm going.
Strange, but I don't
        feel lost.

This dark wood
       seems a waiting place
Waiting for a shaft of sunlight
          to penetrate
               the dense trees
      for rustling footsteps
         to scatter the dry
           autumnal debris.
Waiting for guidance.

Sails Unfurling

When the winds of change
                        begin to sigh
Through my security
Tossing aside the
                comfortable
                        and conventional
Buffeting the *known*,
I resist.

Hoping to avoid risky,
                        uncharted waters
I furl my sails
                tightly,
Clench the rudder
                of my life
In white-knuckled fists
And pretend I'm
                in control.

Eventually
        the uncertain breezes
Inflate my imagination
                with enthusiasm
                        and cautious excitement.
Unfurling my sails
To catch the breath
                of the gale,
I begin to welcome
        the fresh scent of change.

Through the Valley of Divorce

At first
        I wasn't sure
                I'd make it
Money was
        a constant worry
Loneliness,
        a chilling fog.

At first
        I wasn't sure
                I even *cared*
                        if I made it

But, slowly,
        under the guardianship
                of trusted friends,
I garnered
        the courage
                to turn away from the wall
And face my fear

Eventually
        terror turned to security
                resistance became acceptance
        And I even learned to
                enjoy
                        living alone.

Unraveled

The very seams of my soul
Feel frayed by the weight of
                    death
                        business
                            loneliness
I long to collapse in
                angels' arms
And let them gently knit me
Back together

Slowing the Horse

If life
     is a horseback ride
Then I have ridden
       at full gallop
          through its various twists and turns
Occasionally thrown
       to the ground
Where I lay wounded and inert
       face down upon the earth.

As I move into the
       landscape
Of my fifties
I have learned to reign in life
And am leisurely
      walking the path
With periodic kicks
      to the flank
For bursts of speed toward
       known goals.

At this pace I can see
      the texture of my
         surroundings
And truly feel
    the nature
      of my inner world.

I sit comfortably
          in the saddle
Peace of mind
          and contentment
                    as companions.
At least
     for this part of the ride.

The Grace of Work

Although we may not believe it
                    we *need* to work
Indeed a basic yearning
            at our very core
                    is the desire for *meaningful* work.
Through useful tasks
                we have the opportunity
To share the best
            of ourselves
                    with others.

If we malign work as
                a four-letter word
                        or
 a necessary evil that *has* to be done
                            between weekends
                    and always shout
                        "Thank God it's Friday!"
We may need
            different work
                    or
                        different attitudes.

Rocky Places

There are paths that we
                        must each travel alone.
Yours is now sadly strewn
                        with stones.

When you have come to the end
                        I will be there to wash
                                    your wounds
                                        with my tears.

Inner Saboteur

A long time quite demure
My inner saboteur
Has recently come
                bounding to the fore.

Gentle inner voices
Making different choices
"You're bad! Look what you said,
        who you hurt, what you left undone!"
"You're bad! You're bad! You're bad!"

A quick and killing spiral downward.

And now begins
The slow and patient climb up
Crawling, holding, groping, reclaiming,
                remembering, forgiving . . .
Ah, life!

Echoes

Life is good.

My marriage has grown to include
                        more laughter and ease
                                    than judgment.
Responsibilities are few since
The children are mostly
                        on their own.

Success is a grace-filled guest
                        gratitude a constant companion
And I have learned to live in peace
                        with most disappointments.

Why then am I aware of a
                        faint, far-off echo
Am I doing it right?
Is it really okay not to be struggling?

Is there ever a time when that inner voice
                        sings only praises?

My Tutor

Never accommodating
         or overcommitting
For fear she'll be rejected
         or hurt someone's feelings

Sleeping when she's tired
Playing when it suits her
Hunting when she's in the mood
Demanding food when she's hungry
Insisting on
         her own space
And asking for
         what she wants and needs
A purr-fect example of
         assertiveness.

Granted, I would never
         want to be
As slothful and selfish as she
But if I can just learn
A pawful of her independence
I'll be a happier
         more contented me.

Rocking the Boat

Fifty has been a bridge
        from the turbulent seas
                of self-doubt
To the golden pond of self-confidence
                and peace of mind.

Yet even as I sit contentedly
                in my comfy craft
While mirrorlike water reflects
                glorious autumn colors
I recognize an inner tempest
        who yearns to create
                some excitement
By slapping her oars on the surface
Or, more titillating still, tipping over
                the whole damn dinghy!

But the wisdom of these fifty-plus years
                advises me to
Befriend contentment
Instead of allowing
        outgrown patterns
            to rock the boat.

A New Day

Each day is
      a newborn child
Living and dying
        in the scant hours
Between dawn and dusk.

It is our sacred responsibility
To nurture each day,
Unique and precious child
         of our waking hours,
Into the twilight
      of its perfect maturity.

Ripening with Age

Steady Flame

Between youth's raging fires
            of passion and compelling chaos
And old age's cooling embers
                of waning energy and health
Burns the steady flame of midlife
                        warm
                            gentle
                                dependable.

This Old Chassis

Each year
    this old chassis
            is becoming more
  resistant to
            uphill climbs
                    hairpin turns
And being driven
            too hard
                in *any* direction.

She has stopped
            rushing blindly
                    around curves
And is even becoming somewhat patient
                        with detours.

As the miles pile up
            this old chassis
                    needs
            regular maintenance
And a gentle hand
            at the wheel.

Barely Beginning

I'm barely beginning
         to accept
           my own rhythm
Volcanic eruptions
        of creative energy
Followed by
    seemingly fallow periods
        of slow-motion meandering.

Looking back with
        sadness-laced understanding
I realize how I
    lashed my younger self
         mercilessly
For periods of "incorrigible laziness"
Denied the ebbs and flows
      and demanded high-energy output
          always
Pushing
    shoving
      cajoling
        commanding
Never trusting myself to honor
My own rhythm
    for renewal and revitalization.

I'm just now barely beginning
        to gently respect
          my need
For both
    activity and retreat.

Midlife Motto

In lieu of
      "I gotta . . .
            I should . . .
                  I have to . . .
                         EEEEEEEEK!"
This is the motto
        I now speak:

  "I've decided not to worry about that!"

The Peculiarities and Perks of Aging

Somewhere around the age of forty-five
My jawline
           turned to jello
Hot flash no longer meant
                    a news report
And without my glasses
           printed material
                remained a total mystery.

On the other hand

Somewhere around the age of forty-five
I added No
           to my vocabulary
Learned the luxury
           of slowing down
And realized that my children
                had developed
                     into good friends.

Not a bad trade-off.

Wish Full-Filled

In my chaotic
        and out-of-balance
                        youth
I always yearned
        to be well-rounded
"Wish granted!" by the
                    Over-Fifty Fairy
I am well
        and *very* rounded!

Hangin' Loose

We become less uptight after fifty,
                              it's true
And although that's healthier
                      and happier too
Emotions pass the message to
                  our anatomy
"If it's so good for me
              it *must* be good for you"
And our backsides
          downslide.

In Their Own Time

Answers are often slow in coming,
Creeping tortoise-like
              across the busy
Highway of life,
          endangered but unhurried.

We can either dance along the side
Of the road,
        screaming silent, agitated urgings
"Hurry up! What are you waiting for?"
Or we can
Calmly direct traffic
                until the answer is safely
On our side of the road.

Cycles

There is no peace in struggle
                    only growth.

The seed as it sprouts
                    must work through
                              the crust of earth,
Search for sustenance enough
                    to create leaves
                              flowers
                                   fruit
                                        thorns
                                             thistles.

Only after the seed has borne
                    that which it was meant
                              to bear
May it relax and return
                    to its source
Leaving behind other seeds
                    to continue the cycle.
So it is with us.

Once More a Friend

For years food fell
        into disfavor
                because of

Expense:

The constant demand
        to feed
             four ravenous kids
Three cheap, nutritious meals
           which didn't elicit a
"Yuk! Do I *have* to eat this?!"

Guilt:

At throwing together something
        that's only redeeming features
           were speed and simplicity.

Even more guilt:

When hurriedly stopping by McDonalds.

The Weight War:

Teeter-tottering between feelings of
        shame for eating forbidden fruits
          (more likely sugars and starches)
And feelings of resentment and deprivation
        while munching only grapefruit, carrots,
           and cabbage soup.

Now, food is my friend
        because of

Time:

I can browse through the Farmer's Market
        reveling in the color of veggies and flowers
And, in the blessing of spare time,
        enjoy the earthy tasks of washing and
                        arranging my wares.

Expense:

The insatiable teenage appetites,
        which almost prompted me to buy a cow,
Are grazing in their own pastures
                        and
Older eaters are economical.

Guilt:

Who needs it?

The Weight War:

Is in a semi-permanent
        state of cease-fire.

Food,
    beautiful
            sensual
                sustaining
A gift
    to be enjoyed and appreciated

Welcome back, my friend.

At Home

For the first time
        I probably feel better
                on the inside
Than I look
        on the outside.

Over the years
        much energy was expended
                painting and improving
                        my facade
        hoping that, somehow,
                the interior
                    would match up.

Now, though my appearance is showing
                    irreversible signs of aging
    I've uncovered a solid foundation
        that is, more often than not,
                strong
                warm
                    welcoming.

Having crossed the
                threshold of fifty,
I'm able to move more easily
                through *all* the rooms
                        of my interior castle
        with the resources to renovate
                        or redecorate those that need it
        and with grateful acknowledgment
                        of those that are okay as is.

At home with myself
                at last.

Mother, Is That You?

One day while glancing
                    in the mirror
I saw a familiar face.
      "Mother, what on earth are you doing here,
            for I am young and you are old!"
With a shocked expression
                    the same as my own
She gasped,
      "*That* hasn't been true for years, my dear!"

MenoPause

Feeling sexy
I, wearing my glasses,
Found, for the first time,
      white pubic hairs
Below my hormone patch . . .

For a moment,
      desire faded.

Junk Food Junkies

Before we cared
    about cholesterol
        high blood pressure
          or tooth-decaying plaque
We were dedicated
      junk food junkies.

    If it wasn't served in a
            logo-ed sack
    and didn't give us a
           hypoglycemic attack
    If it wasn't covered with mustard
             in a bun
    and wouldn't make us gain
        close to a ton
    If it wasn't gooey and chewy
        and chocolate too
    Then I didn't want it
    and neither did you!

If it couldn't be sipped through
                              colored straws
or eaten while we held it in
                    our hot little paws
If it wasn't greasy and gave us
                         a pimple or two
Then I didn't want it
and neither did you!

But now that midlife
                    includes mid-spread
And caffeine causes
                  a sleepless bed
We've become exercising
                     juice drinking
                                broccoli fans
With nary a Big Mac
              greasing our hands.

Gravity

Even as my face
            has fallen
So has fallen away
            layers of
Rigid, imprisoning
            should's and *have to's.*

Gravity, an enemy to my looks,
In compensation has allowed
            to slip, slide, and gather
In an unused heap
            around my feet
Insecurity
        and the need
            to please all of the people
                all of the time.

While the law of gravity
            inflicts its natural consequences
                upon my body
The attitude of gravity,
        a weighty and ever so serious view of life,
Is being replaced by
            lightness of heart,
                confidence in my credibility,
And measureless gratitude.

I welcome the patina of age
For the priceless inner jewels
            it reveals.

Invasion of AARP

I was doing great . . .

    "Not bad for an old broad!"
                          I preened,

   "Pretty spry for the half-century mark, m'dear!"
       I crowed,
               barely perspiring after
                         aerobics class.

But the United States mail
                 shattered my
                     illusion of youth
When—unsolicited—I received
              my AARP card.
Now, how the hell did
    the American Association of Retired Persons
                       know that
I was over fifty?

A Better Tomorrow

Today is like a white hot
                    coal of pain
Right in your gut
Will tomorrow be better?
Maybe not
But in several
                or maybe many
                            tomorrows
Life will be better
                than it ever was
I know
Because I have been where
                    you are today.

The Macho God of Menopause

It's official . . .
The god of
      menopause
Is definitely
      male!

No feminine deity
Would subject
      a grown woman
To the erratic and irrational feelings
      of a pubescent girl
  or the full-body flushes
      of sleep-disrupting
        hot flashes
  or the horror
      of suddenly stained
        below-the-waist-wear.
No . . .

The god of
      menopause
Is definitely
      male,
And I have lain
      awake nights
Alternately
    roasting in a forty-degree room
      and freezing in my own clammy sweat
Plotting
    my revenge!

Voices

We can run from
              external voices
Which assail
        deride
              and torment us.
Those we can escape.

But inner voices
We must
     transform
In order to gain
           peace of mind.

We cannot bolt
            fast enough
To elude
      dodge
           or evade
Enemies
     carried within.
Those we must
          befriend
In order to gain
           peace of mind.

An Eye for an Eye

Eyes that can no longer read
                without assistance
Often focus keenly
                on inner visions
        of beauty
                simplicity
                        and truth.

As outward sight
            dwindles,
                    inner vision may sharpen.
Illusive glimpses
            of creation's
                        awe-inspiring wonder
        once eclipsed by external dazzle
Now become a perpetual panorama
                        of grateful
                            awareness.

Reaping the Harvest
of Relationships

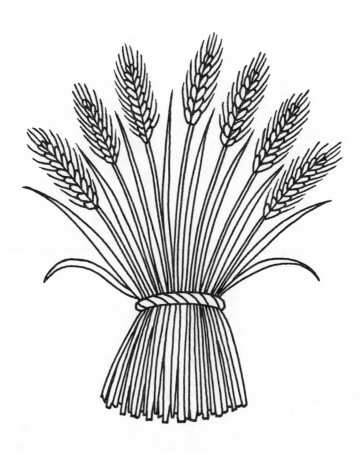

Love's Garlands

Before the mystery
            of our love
I can merely bow,
And offer garlands
            of gratitude!

Autumn of Motherhood

In a burst of fiery beauty,
        yet gently and graciously,
Autumn disrobes her trees
Freeing them from the work
        of maintaining
                nurturing
                    and supporting
    their mantle of leaves.

Starkly silhouetted against
            the winter sky
Trees are invited to return
To the strength of their roots
                    to rest
Gathering energy for
    next season's budding and blossoming.

So it is with motherhood.

As our children cling tenaciously
To the last bare branch
        of the empty nest
Or drop excitedly from the tree
            which bore them
Exploding into glorious color
        with the flame of their
                independence,

Our task is to
        lovingly
              kindly
                    gently
Let go
  and return to the strength
                of *our* roots
                        to rest.

And Then They Were Equal

The days of your kingship
                    have passed
So don't shellac me with your
                    should's and *ought's*.

Judging, withdrawal, righteous indignation
Will no longer be met with
                    automatic contrition
Acceptance of all blame
And pleadings for approval
          from lowly Cinderella.

I've grown up.

Judging, withdrawal, and righteous indignation
Will now be met with apology
                    if deserved
Real feelings—*even anger*—
Limits and boundaries
And sharing of responsibility.

So abdicate your throne
As I have relinquished my place
                    among the ashes
And together, as partners,
We can
     share the load
               pull the cart
                    and smell the roses.

Not riding into the sunset
To live happily ever after
But going toward our sunset years
Dear friends and lovers
Caring
        laughing
                learning
                        and growing
Both together and apart.

Love Disarmed

Do we meet our loved ones
Armed
    with sharp words
        and a keen wit
Or greet them
Disarmingly
    with gentle ears
        and an open mind?

There is a place for
        well-honed sharpness
But rarely is it
    in close relationships.

Illness Awareness

For the first time since
                    I've known him
My husband looks old.

The weeks of pain
                have accumulated weightily
                            in his feet
Creating an unfamiliar shuffle
As he slowly walks
                to the drinking fountain
To take a pill.

My heart silently screams
                in protest
Longing to erase the weariness
Hurry the healing
And resurrect the vital, enthusiastic
Youthful man he is
                when pain-free.

Seeing him like this
Jerks me face-to-face
With the terrifying realization
                that we will be separated
                                by death
Sooner or later.

Oh God,
Please let it be
                later!

Garden-Variety Family

In the garden
               a riot of wildflowers
Bright,
      open-faced,
            aggressive blooms
                  boldly announce their presence
While soft,
   demure,
      secretive blossoms
         remain almost hidden beneath the clover.

Their diversity
            reminds me of my own
                 garden-variety family.
All of us present such
          different faces
              to the world

While each reseeds the landscape
             in his or her own
                strikingly unique way.

God's Joke, a Generalization . . .

To create two totally
                different realities
        and make them irresistibly
                    drawn to each other . . .
    logical
            linear
                conquering male;
    intuitive
            feeling
                relating female!

Luckily, Spirit shook
                the primordial bag a bit
Dusting us with at least
                    a tinge
                        of *all* qualities . . .
        enough to make a
            respectable attempt at
                    understanding each other.

Ultimately
        accepting and celebrating
                        our differences
Seems the best way
                to have the last laugh.

Yet Another Change

The "boys" shower us with grins
                from the cab
Of the rented
        moving van
Young, handsome, vibrant—
Expectant faces
            dreaming
                of fresh adventures
Eager to conquer
           the miles
Between them and
         their new lives.

We "girls,"
My daughter and I,
Cling to each other
            tummies bumping
Sobbing out our grief
         at yet another change.

Our family is scattering
And will never be
         the same.

The men look outward
Focusing on what's next
           seemingly forgetting the old
Letting go without
         a backward glance

While we women nurture within
Memories of what has been
Appreciating and cherishing the creation
                              of our family
Feeling the pain
            of giving birth
                        to the new.

They are not wrong
            and we are not right
It is just another example
                  of how differently
                              we view
Yet another change.

Sister of My Soul

Before I met you
There was a RESERVED sign
On the corner table of my heart
Reserved for
           a heart-sister

When we first came face-to-face
It was apparent that spot
Was saved for you

No one had before
                has now
                        or ever will have
Your special place,
                sister of my soul

Treasures

Life has given me
          many gifts
You and the children
          are my most treasured.

The kids go through me
          toward life
You go with me
     through life.

The Niagara Falls of Parenthood

Like a river rushing willingly over a waterfall
As concerned parents
We pour our best
        onto our kids
Who clutch our offerings ravenously
             in their hands
  and, without a backward glance,
           race headlong
              downstream
Where, hopefully, they will one day
Pour *their* best onto
        our grandchildren.

Expecting water, or selfless love,
          to flow any other way
Is bucking
    the current!

The Changing Skyline

The skyline of
             my relationships
Is ever-changing
Many whom I love so dearly
Are no longer silhouetted
             against my horizon
Gone forever
Through death's one-way door
Other of my loves are
             out of reach
Across untouchable miles

Today I miss them deeply
And a melancholy fog of sadness
Obscures my usually
             cheerful outlook.

Cease-Fire

If there is such a thing
        as the war between the sexes
Then as a teenager
        I yearned to be recruited
Sacrificing many personal beliefs
        on the altar of popularity.

But the serious bombing began
        in my twenties
When I surrendered into
        "What he says, goes"
  and lost both the battle
        and the man.

Love disarmed my
        tightly defended thirties.
Armistice
    blessed the days,
Yet secret shelling
        bombarded the darkness
While I struggled to hold on to
        ideals of
        equality and partnership.

Embattled,
    fatigued by capitulation
        contrition
        and peace at any price,

I exploded into my forties
   daring masculine mortars
      to invade.
Independence my motto
    justice my creed
       visibility my promise,
I marched
  with clenched fists,
     eventually winning a truce.

Sheltered in the confidence of my fifties,
   a compassionate cease-fire
     enfolds both myself
       and the men in my life.

A Priceless Gift

A true friend
    brings out the best in us
While knowing the worst.
Even though privileged
       to our ugliest inner toads,
A true friend believes in
       our goodness
         our worth
Our ability to
     survive and thrive.

A true friend
    acts as a confessional
      in which we can
        purge out guilt
   and a kiln in which we
      fire our strength.

A Mother's Heart

A mother's heart is
                never closed
The welcome mat is
                always out
For her children,
                prodigal or present.

A mother's heart is
                always open
Willing and wanting
                relationship and reconciliation.

No wound is too deep
No division too wide
To close a mother's heart
                                forever.

Safe Spiral

The ever-evolving spiral
                    of our love
Embraces individuality
                    and difference of opinion
Balanced with the security
                    of history and commitment.
Feelings fluctuate
            fear and certainty
                    mourning and rejoicing
                        struggle and ease
                            anger and appreciation
Ebb and flow
            the natural rhythm and progression
                    of a dynamic partnership.

But almost always
                there is gentle
                        safety
In the circle
            of each other's
                        arms.

Possibilities

I love what is now
        and what can be
                    limitless
                        growing
                            sharing

Becoming richer
            deeper
                more meaningful

An unfolding tapestry
            weaving and reaching the interior
                        of self and loved one

An exciting exploration of
                who we were
                    who we are
                        who we can become
Individually and together.

Heart's Anchor

The older I become
                the more I value
My women friends.

Our hearts
          hands
                and hugs
Sustain each other
     through the thistles
               and burning deserts
                         of grief and crisis
And stand ready to applaud and laugh
               when there is joy and triumph
                         to be celebrated.

Enduring friendships—
                shared history and hilarity—
Anchor me
     in my reality
And buoy me
     for the continuing
                    quest.

Who's in Charge?

Who's in charge
When he stands silent, tall,
                and awesomely cold?

Who's in charge
When she whimpers and whines,
                begging to be comforted?

Who's in charge . . .

Not the kind and thoughtful man
Nor the caring, creative woman

Who's in charge . . .

Two children
                lost among the goblins
Of their fear.

From the vantage point
                of maturity
We can now recognize
                those inner children
Recess to comfort the fearful
And reconvene when
Compassion
                can be in charge.

With Love

Without love
> the sky is not as blue
>> nor flowers quite as fresh

Without love
> adventures lose their zest
>> and goals seem less important

Without love
> confidence wanes
> and creativity dwindles

Without love
> breath is not as deep
>> nor hearts as open

Strengthened by love,
> both given and received,
Our spirits can soar
> to unimagined heights
Encouraging us to
> become who we are
>> meant to be.

Gathering the Fruits
of the Vine

Drinking from the Well

Water

Without it
       the body dies
              so quickly.

Solitude

Without it
       the soul withers
              so quietly.

Living Poetically

Living poetically

An economy of
       word
           action
               and distraction

Walking in beauty

Simply
      quietly
           lovingly
               enthusiastically

Serenity Interruptus

Although I desire to sink
              into the peaceful waters
                            of silence,
My thoughts, like unruly corks,
              keep popping to
                            the surface
   making waves and wobbles on
              what I hoped would be
                   undisturbed calm and serenity.
How to "decork" my mind?

Paintings from an Inner Palette

Pristine, virgin canvas
                    waiting
For the artistry only I can create.
Abundant hues, tints, and tones
An infinite inner palette
                    from which to choose.
Deep, dramatic vermilion
Lining the passage of my days
                    with bursts of fiery passion.
Soothing Persian blue
Azure yearning for long-forgotten
                            mysteries.
Energized, creative, buttercup yellow
Impatient to splash the canvas
                    with swatches of brilliant
                            change and growth.
The comfort of healing emerald green
Softening struggles and pain with shades of nature.
For emphasis and contrast, dashes of ebony
Black grief and depression
                        enhancing appreciation
For the canvas as a whole.

Wisdom is knowing
Where to leave the canvas untouched,
Pure, undefiled space
Waiting to welcome the Divine.

All of the canvas is ours to paint,
                our creation
                        our colors
                                our life.

Rx for Healing

Spirituality
Self-love
Silence
Simplicity
Service

Gently Down the Stream

As the song
        reminds us,
Row gently
Down the stream

Do not
     thrash frantically
Up against the current.

Gently
     gently
Glide with
       events and circumstances.
Resistance only
       magnifies pain.

Ride the tides
Gently
     gracefully
         with acceptance.

Sister Moon

Moonlight
        gentle
                cool
                        friendly
Flowing from
        the shining
                        feminine circle
Ever changing
Yet dependable
                predictable
We set our calendars
                by her cycles
And lift our faces
                for the caress
Of her blessing.

Bathed in moonlight
We are carried
        into a knowing
                        a comfort
A deep sense of
                connectedness
                        with the All

Nightly
        and forever
She smiles her benediction
                upon her sister, Earth,
And upon us,
        our Mother's children.

Pollination

Opening
    as a flower
        to a bee
Buttercup face
    raised to the sun

  Help me be a light-bearer.

    Thy will, not mine.

      You through me.

The Retreat of the Higher Self

Tell me where you hide
When nights are short
               and days harried
To what sanctuary
          do you retreat
When others' incessant voices
              fill each interior room
  and solitude exists
           only in wavering memory?

Tell me where you go . . .
    to gallop among the Ancients?
    to sit by the eternal river?
    or merely, to sleep?

No matter where you disappear
              when circumstances
              or lack of will
                 create neglect and exile
Thankfully, you always return
When I sincerely
          invite your wisdom
              to guide my life.

Please tell me how to *consistently*
              keep you near!

Soul Retrieval

My heart aches for the
                busy young women
Who have no time for silence,
Their days filled
                with the chatter of children
                        the clatter of computers
                                and the clamor of demands.

Where does a young woman's
                        soul go?
Where did my own go
When I was young and overly busy?

Into retirement.

Perhaps the work of midlife and beyond
                        is really soul retrieval.

Vintage

The older the
            vine
The sweeter the
            grape.

Homing

We are all free spirits
Souls on our own paths
                    toward oneness.
Other beings may influence us
But the journey is
                    ours alone.
The path,
          our choice
The destination,
                our decision.

Some enter this adventure of life
As light-bearers
While others trail shadows
                        heavy with pain
But each soul, at its center,
                          is wise
Capable of finding
                its own way
Home.

Personal Note

In my introduction, I invited you to send me examples of your own writing. I mean it! I would love to hear from you. I hope *Autumn of the Spring Chicken* helps you celebrate all of the varied aspects of ripening with age and blooming into your best self. To share poems or experiences, or receive autographed copies of THE WOMAN'S BOOK OF CONFIDENCE, THE WOMAN'S BOOK OF COURAGE, or THE COURAGE TO BE YOURSELF, please write to me:

Sue Patton Thoele
P.O. Box 1519
Boulder, CO 80306-1519

Liberate the Creative Crone in You!

Join Creative Crone Consultants *Un*Limited (a completely unofficial, hang-loose unorganization of magical, mature women). Simply send a stamped self-addressed envelope to me at the above address to receive your own personal membership card.